MORDECHAI ANIELEWICZ:

NO

TO DESPAIR

MORDECHAI ANIELEWICZ:

NO
TO DESPAIR

RACHEL HAUSFATER

Translated by ALISON L. STRAYER

THEY SAID NO SERIES EDITOR, MURIELLE SZAC

Triangle Square Books for Young Readers
Seven Stories Press
NEW YORK • OAKLAND • LONDON

Seven Stories Press
www.sevenstories.com

Library of Congress Cataloging-in-Publication Data

Names: Hausfater, Rachel, author. | Strayer, Alison L., translator.
Title: Mordechai Anielewicz : no to despair / Rachel Hausfater ; translated
  by Alison L. Strayer.
Other titles: Mordechai Anielewicz. English | No to despair
Description: New York : Triangle Square Books for Young Readers / Seven
  Stories Press, [2022] | Series: They said no | Original title "Mordechai
  Anielewicz" published in French. | Audience: Ages 10-14 years. |
  Summary: Follows the final days of Mordechai Anielewicz, leader of the
  Jewish Fighting Organization that led the insurrection against Nazi
  control in Poland during the Holocaust.
Identifiers: LCCN 2022011244 | ISBN 9781644211328 (paperback) | ISBN
  9781644211335 (electronic)
Subjects: LCSH: Anielewicz, Mordecai, 1919-1943--Juvenile fiction. |
  Jews--Poland--Juvenile fiction. | CYAC: Anielewicz, Mordecai,
  1919-1943--Fiction. | Jews--Poland--Fiction. | Holocaust, Jewish
  (1939-1945)--Poland--Fiction. | World War, 1939-1945--Underground
  movements--Fiction. | World War, 1939-1945--Poland--Fiction. | Warsaw
  (Poland)--History--Warsaw Ghetto Uprising, 1943--Fiction. |
  Poland--History--Occupation, 1939-1945--Fiction. | LCGFT: Biographical
  fiction. | Historical fiction.
Classification: LCC PZ7.1.H3874 Mo 2022 | DDC [E]--dc23
LC record available at https://lccn.loc.gov/2022011244

Cover illustration: François Roca

College professors and high school and middle school teachers may order free
examination copies of Seven Stories Press titles. Visit https://www.sevenstories.
com/pg/resources-academics or email academics@sevenstories.com.

Printed in the USA.

9 8 7 6 5 4 3 2 1

My thanks to the team at the Shoah Memorial of Paris for their welcome and accessibility.

All the chapter titles and quotes at the beginnings of chapters are words spoken or written by Mordechai Anielewicz or other combatants of the ghetto.

The "ch" of Mordechai is pronounced with a very guttural "h" sound in the back of the throat (as in the Spanish word *jota* or the Hebrew word *challah*).

*"The opposite of
despair is not hope,
it's struggle."*

MORDECHAI ANIELEWICZ

Contents

1

"We Don't Want to Save Our Lives"

We don't want to save our lives.
Nobody gets out alive.
We only want to save our human dignity.

Mordechai Anielewicz speaks.

The angel Mordechai.

He speaks, and calmly declares war.

April 18, 1943. Evening already, maybe our last. Outside it's so dark but there's a light inside us, an ardent little fire lit by him, our sweet commander.

He speaks and everyone listens, because he's our leader, the one with the vision, will, and ability to lead us far away from here in glory and in beauty. So we can go with pride, go standing, strike out at death, live right up to the final moment.

The final moment is now, and tomorrow is the end.

Around Mordechai Anielewicz stand his five commanders.

Put together, their ages barely total one hundred and ten, and their soldiers are children of thirteen, seventeen, or twenty. Mordechai is twenty-four and he's the oldest. Twenty-four is young to be old, to be a leader, to know. But it's really not such a short time because these days life doesn't last. For us it will end tomorrow, in three days, a week, or maybe a month if the miracle occurs, the one Mordechai is talking about: the miracle of weapons, and of us, as attackers, assailants, fighters; the miracle of Germans fleeing, losing, of Germans dying.

Mordechai speaks and his words enlighten us, because his words are simple and strong. He says that we're going to fight without help, almost without weapons. That of course we'll lose, but our honor will be saved. He says we'll die but we'll die alive.

Everyone feels it and everyone knows: our struggle is hopeless.

But when Mordechai speaks, he kills despair.

2

"It Is Impossible to Describe the Conditions"

*It is impossible to describe the
conditions in the ghetto. Very few will be able
to endure them. All others are destined to
perish, sooner or later.*

And yet, our situation is so desperate! We've been living (or hanging on to life) locked up in this ghetto prison for two and a half years, since the autumn of 1940.

A year before that, the Germans invaded Poland and persecuted us a little more each day. And then they decided to lock up all the Jews of Warsaw and the surrounding areas, four hundred thousand poor human beings herded like animals into a too-small walled, overcrowded, and unsanitary neighborhood. Forbidden to leave, with almost nothing to eat, exposed to the cold, diseases, and the Nazis who kill. Corpses in the streets, ashen-faced children, weeping, wailing, fear that never ends. Surrounded by walls and the Germans' weapons. Cornered, trapped, doomed. Perishing by the thousands. And yet hoping to not die, to get out, to be saved, hoping for freedom.

But when? Freed by whom? How?

"To revolt is dangerous, they'll take our children. It's better to obey, wait, lie low, not turn against those who are so powerful. They can't kill us all, impossible! If they deport us, it's probably to work. Don't listen to those young hotheads who talk about resistance and armed struggle, they're putting us in danger, they'll get us all killed!"

That's what people say, while all around us the cold, hunger, and typhus kill so many, so many. That's what people think, all this time refusing to see and believe what's going to happen.

Until the summer and the great Aktion that is meant to eliminate us. Because for the Germans, we don't die enough or fast enough. They want more of us dead, they want us all dead.

They closed the streets, arrested everyone, forced us to walk to the Umschlagplatz and put us on trains, crammed into cattle cars. They had so many weapons and we only our bare hands! How were we supposed to resist? And what about little children?

And besides, maybe when we arrived, who knows, we might have a few more days, a little more life . . .

But they deported us to black death camps where they gassed us, burned us, murdered us. Slaughtered us by the millions.

Everyone knows, everyone has seen. This is what Mordechai says.

That there, the ovens burn, gas asphyxiates, and Jews, all the Jews, are disappearing, vanishing into the air.

That's what they're doing to us, that's how

we're going to go. Up in flames, in smoke, denied, annihilated. As if we'd never existed.

3

"We're Not Fighting for Life"

We're not fighting for life, but for the price of life;
not to avoid death, but to choose the way in which we'll die.

Unless we decide on another way to end.

And thereby to exist and shine forever.

You can't choose to live, not in 1942 when you're a Jew in Poland and the Nazis are there. But Mordechai says we can at least choose how we'll die, and what we'll die for. That's what he proposes, a clean and noble death, death in combat for the sake of honor, Jewish honor. We'll go to war for our dignity, and it doesn't matter if we die, for it will be saved.

The opposite of despair is not hope.

It's struggle.

For that we need weapons, and there aren't

any. We have to go outside the ghetto to find them, buy them from the Poles who don't want to help us. So we send fighters to the other side to search, beg, urge, negotiate. And then runners who will go back and forth smuggling letters, provisions, guns.

That's what I am, Feigele: a little messenger girl, a former smuggler. Mordechai recruited me one evening when I was slipping under the wall, a stubborn little mole, so loaded down I could barely stand up. It was the end of '41, and I was only twelve years old. I came by every day to exchange abandoned objects for food, over, under, or through the wall, working stones loose and scraping at the earth. That evening, at dusk, the hour between dog and wolf, between dogs and wolves, I was coming back with a bag of bread around my neck and potatoes stuffed down the legs of my pants, tied at the bottom. I was so loaded down that I couldn't get out of the hole, and I was struggling, and the soldiers were coming, and death was approaching . . . When

I saw a hand reaching out to me, I didn't know whether it meant to kill or expose or just rob me. But when I looked up, I saw a thin, pale young man, a serious student in threadbare clothes, with black hair and dark green eyes that seemed to smile at me in the midst of their sadness.

I saw an angel.

So I took his hand and never let go of it again.

4

"Fight, Die for Honor"

Fight, die for honor. Jewish honor!

Quick! We run, hide, eat, and then talk. We exchange names. I tell him where I come from and what I do, but not him; he says almost nothing but is a very good listener and asks the right questions. Then the words in me that want to overflow spill out all at once. I tell him about my beautiful life before, when all my people were alive, my cheerful parents, a beautiful little brother, grandparents, aunts and uncles, lots of cousins, good neighbors. I loved life so much, when I had one, the trees in the park, my sunny room full of books I'd read cover to cover, the piano playing, bright-colored dresses and big fresh cakes. And then thunder, war, fear, the ghetto, filth, and being shut in. The books sold, the piano burned, the dresses torn, and the stomach empty. And then the grandfather gone, friends disappeared, and Mama falling out of bed all the time, slowly dying, dying and leaving me behind. And then last month, my little lost brother: his name was Motek, he was only four, such a wonderful child, a brother so delightful, sunny laughter, magnificent dreams. But his face grew hollow, he lost his joy, there was nothing left of him but his eyes that screamed, his hands that pleaded. I held him, I shook him so he wouldn't fall asleep, I carried him until I fell so that he would start to move again. But in my arms there was nothing left but a little pile of rags with a dead face that no longer had a name.

I didn't save him but I tried!

"You didn't save him, but you can avenge him," says Mordechai, who listens to me weep, his eyes too brimming with sorrow.

Avenge him? But how? I'm just a child . . .

He laughs and says: "A child? So what? When I was your age, I fought all the time!"

It's his turn to tell his story and I listen. I see him, little Mordechai, six years old, so poor and yet so lighthearted, joyful, and full of energy, who played for hours in the streets and courtyards of his miserable district of Warsaw. He was friends with everyone—Jews, Poles, what did it matter? Except when they said: "We like you, you're not like the other dirty Yids!" Then his blood boiled, his anger flared, furious he rushed at them and hit them, weeping, not understanding but cut to the quick by the insult. His rage was so intense and sudden that despite his frail body and young age, he emerged victorious with a bloody nose and black eyes, but his honor avenged, the tiny burning honor of a humiliated little Jewish boy.

Over the years, the insults became more vicious, and fights better organized. Regularly, when making deliveries for his father's grocery store with his brother or coming back from school with his friends, gangs of thugs attacked them, trying to break the Jews. They showered them with insults and beat them up. There were a great many Polish boys and they were armed, so the young Jews often came home wounded, their clothes in tatters and their pride in shreds. Until the day that Mordechai, with his brother's help, lured one of the thugs away from the others and gave him such a beating that afterward, people were afraid of Mordechai and left him alone.

Time passed. Not much time. Then of course it began again. So he began again too. You had to survive, you had to be respected.

And when the punishing attacks began on Jewish homes in the area (punishment for what? All they'd done was live there . . .), he and his friends formed a gang to protect residents and give the anti-Semitic gangs a dignified welcome with clubs, stones, and brass knuckles.

I look at him with amazement. You'd never

believe, to see him so gentle, that he was a fighter and made people bleed.

"But I didn't like it," he confesses. "I preferred to read and go to school. My father wanted me to start working, but my mother insisted that I keep at my studies. I loved to learn and I did well, especially in history and literature. I even learned Hebrew on my own! And in the evening I gave courses to whoever wanted them to pay for my books and a less shabby jacket . . ."

Yet, when he had to, and that was often, he fought and he won. I want that too, to act instead of crying, to strike out without running away, to kill killers and avenge the small victims of massacre. So when he asks me to work for him, carrying messages and smuggling packages, being part of their struggle, that of Mordechai and his friends, I say yes, of course, oh yes, because I want to be like him, do as he does, be worthy of him.

Mordechai, even as a child, was a resistance fighter!

5

"Don't Get Used to It!"

Don't get used to it!
Rebel against reality!

I see him every day. I watch him in the court-yards, I call hello and he always answers. I obey his orders, do everything he says; I run, carry, smuggle, hide, and then slip away. He teaches me how not to get caught or lose my life or my precious cargo. On the other side of the wall, so many dangers lie in wait for us, the Germans, of course, but also Polish Jew-hunters who want to turn us in, so we have to give them money, or escape, or, better still, go unnoticed. But to do that, we have to hide our eyes that betray us, too hungry, too unhappy. When we pass to the other side, the eyes must not be Jewish.

But how do you hide your eyes? How do you hide your sorrow? How do you not despair?

With action, of course, and by fighting together. By watching Mordechai I learn. Because he's an example, he resists all the time.

Day after day, and even at night, he prepares his war without weapons and without fighters. He organizes his troops, seeks outside help, educates, trains, explains. Tirelessly he talks with people to convince them that they have to fight, to accept nothing, and to not give up. He takes care of the "whispered propaganda," writing pamphlets and newspaper articles, pasting up posters to rouse the Jews, call them to combat, urge them to disobedience. And he also fights physically, like before; early one morning, when police burst into his room, ordering him to get up and come with them so they can send him to a labor camp, he makes as if to obey and then pounces, hitting them with all his might, and escapes, victorious. Nobody can stop him.

He could have left; Mordechai Anielewicz

could have fled, saved his life. He had contacts, networks, and friends. When there was still time, he could have left Poland and made his way to the country of his dreams, settled in Palestine and built Israel there. But do you leave a burning land? Do you run away alone when others will perish? Do you abandon your people to despair? Do you give up the fight?

Not he, no, never. Because he's not in it for himself, he's in it for the others. He wants to do for, be with, fight against.

He rejects everything that comes out of evil, terror, death, and deportation, but also humiliation. He says no to enslavement, no to German orders, to demeaning rules. For him nothing is harmless; he doesn't compromise, anything that humiliates and tramples people must not be accepted. He no longer wears a cap since Jews must remove their hats when passing Germans as a sign of submission, and too bad if the winter cold is biting. He simply lets his hair grow to cover his head a little. But he's not really cold: dignity keeps you warm.

He resists everything, even stupidity, and the most important thing of all is to always be on the alert! Despite the brutal life, the sordid daily existence and the future so bleak it looks like death, his mind is still razor-edged, his thinking brilliant, and his thirst for learning insatiable. So Mordechai reads late at night after meetings, books on history, economics, and sociology, and he feels his human spirit spread its wings and fly free.

Learning and teaching are what he's always done. From the age of fifteen, in the Hashomer Hatzair, a socialist Zionist* youth movement, he shared his passion for Jewish culture and social justice with other young people. He gave lessons in Hebrew, history, and philosophy, and devoted so much time to political activism that his parents grew desperate. "Behave like a good Jewish boy," his father scolded him. "Do something with your life," his mother begged him.

And that's what he's doing!

---

* Zionism: a political movement that supports the creation of a Jewish state in Palestine.

6

"Remember How We Were Betrayed"

Remember how we were betrayed.
The day will come when we'll take revenge
for all the innocent blood that was shed.

He's not alone, of course. All around him and by his side are wonderful, passionate young people, these boys and girls, resistance fighters like him. All, or nearly all, are members of youth movements, Zionist, socialist, or Bundist*—idealists. Before the war they campaigned for equality and fraternity, dreamed of the Jewish country they'd build in Palestine. They learned Hebrew, read Marx and Trotsky, discussed, argued, demon-

---

* Bundism: a Jewish socialist movement born in Russia in the late nineteenth century

strated. Tomorrow would be glorious, their revolution would be in a united world, they would pick oranges on the hills of Zion. No more discrimination or anti-Semitism, no more very poor or very rich, everyone would be brothers and sisters. Until then they would sing and dance and fall in love.

But now that tomorrow has arrived, there's no revolution or liberation. Instead of the Promised Land they find themselves trapped in a land that is doomed. Dreams of a new world where all would be equal, a new country that would finally be theirs, are all so distant. They wanted to build, but everything they hoped for was destroyed. They wanted everyone to love one another, but the world hates them. Their tomorrows no longer sing, they cry out and moan. And the future that seemed so vast, full, and rich, withers and contorts as it dies in agony.

Yet they don't despair, they continue to struggle. Shut up in the ghetto in the middle of a suffering people, they devote their too short youth to making life more human—feeding, caring for, educating, and entertaining. And making death more human—getting ready, training, rebelling, resisting.

Around Mordechai there are people who are wonderful and full of life.

But during the great and terrifying Aktion of the summer of 1942, around us it seems as if there are only poor, dying people.

Between July 22 and September 13, the ghetto is emptied of nearly three hundred thousand of its occupants. Every day eight thousand to ten thousand babies, little boys and girls, teenagers, young people, mothers and fathers, men and women, old gentlemen and elderly ladies are deported to Treblinka, sorted, stripped, gassed, and then burned. In a crowd, in a line, and in the end, on fire.

A whole people sacrificed, slaughtered almost entirely. Those who are sent to find out what's happening return staggering and vomiting with horror, sobbing as they repeat what they saw, what they smelled, what they understood: the silence in the camp, the trains leaving again, and the odor, the odor of abject death. It truly looks as if this is the end of us.

In any case, it's the end of what remains of my family.

The day when they are rounded up, I'm away on a mission and arrive too late—but too late for what? To save them or go with them? In our over-crowded street, panic-stricken, cornered people stumble and cry out and search. They keep moving, alas, for where are they supposed to go? They obey, of course, because they're unarmed. And suddenly I see them, my family, the only people I had, the last who loved me, and they're being taken to their deaths and all I can do is watch, weeping brutal tears that have no right to flow. They walk, my poor people, when they should be running. "Save yourselves! Fight!" I want to shout. My little cousins whimper, my grandmother falls and doesn't get up, my aunts are dazed and my uncles expressionless. I see my father, so handsome, still tall and shining, he's leaving without me, Papa, wait! But he's seen me too and tips his hat in farewell because he wants me to live and is forcing me to stay. So I obey him, I say nothing, I step back, I let them go, never to see them again.

I've lost all my kin, and now there's nobody left who knows what I was like as a child.

The only family I have left is Mordechai and his people.

My people.

7

"The Time Is Coming"

*The time is coming. You have to be
ready to fight back. Not a single Jew must
leave on the trains. Let's all get
ready to die like men.*

In September, the Aktion ends, but we know there'll be another, and that it will be the last. Then, like a fever that has spread to us all, the fight becomes really organized, this time with the support of the ghetto population. The few people remaining have understood that to obey kills, that the trains are death trains and the only hope is in revolt. In the following months, the sixty thousand surviving Jews dig bunkers and tunnels, set up hideouts, and gather supplies. They prepare their defense.

Meanwhile, Mordechai Anielewicz and his fighters prepare their attack.

In November 1942, Mordechai is appointed commander of the Jewish Combat Organization (JCO), which brings together all branches of the resistance. The JCO oversees all aspects of survival in the ghetto, and actively prepares for insurrection. Which will soon happen—when, we don't know, but we need weapons, and help that doesn't come. We can't fight with our bare hands!

Mordechai sends emissaries out of the ghetto to try to convince the Armia Krajowa, the Polish resistance, to sell us weapons and support our struggle. But they make us beg, they hesitate, discuss, delay, and in the end let us have only a few pistols that cost us a fortune. When they have so many! And when we're fighting the Germans just like them! It almost looks as if it hurts them to arm us, as if they don't want to help us and couldn't care less if we die. Isn't it the same struggle? Don't we have the same enemy? Aren't we the same, them and us?

"No, for them, we're not the same," Mordechai answers. "War or no war, the Polish really don't like us." And he tells me about his brief stay in the summer of 1937 at a paramilitary training camp, organized by the Polish army for high school students. He and his Jewish friends had immediately been set apart in a separate tent, and when the Polish boys laughed at them, calling them weaklings unable to fight and wage war, they clenched their fists in silence. But the day their training weapons were stolen, Mordechai lost what little patience he had and prepared a surprise attack. The next night, they stormed the culprits' tent, beat them up and forced them to run away half naked. Of course, Mordechai was expelled from the camp as a troublemaker, but he didn't care, he was satisfied. They'd avenged themselves, they'd shown them how Jews fight!

Since nothing has changed and the Polish resistance doesn't want to share—not even war—with us, we must rely on mobsters, thieves, smugglers, people who don't ask what the weapons will be used for or by whom. Except these people are hard to find, they try to cheat you, ask for so much money and give so little in return, too often disappear, and are liable to turn us in. Still, little by little, our arsenal grows. If only little by little . . .

I'm not an emissary, of course, I'm too young, but still I'm part of this sacred quest. I smuggle out the money used to pay bribes, accomplices, blackmailers, to pay for hideouts and weapons. I carry messages to fighters staked out in apartments outside the ghetto, responsible for contacts and purchases. I return to the ghetto with their replies and packages of things to eat . . . or to kill with. I feel powerful when I carry the heavy, important weight of a pistol, ammunition, or equipment. And how proud I am the day I'm given the task of bringing back dynamite wrapped in greasy paper! I know how dangerous it is and I'm afraid of blowing up. But I also know how precious it is and I'm afraid of failing in my mission. On the way back, I run gently, climb carefully, cradle my package like a baby, hug it against me like a treasure. And when I finally get past the wall and arrive at Mordechai's headquarters, trembling and proud, everyone cries out in joy and congratulates me, shaking my hand as if I were a soldier, and they're already calculating all the explosives we'll be able to make. Only Mordechai hangs back; he looks at me with sorrow, ruffles my hair with his slender hand, and softly says: "Little child, you could have died . . . To think it was me who sent you . . ." But I say thank you, we cannot regret, we cannot hesitate, I'm not a child, I'm thirteen and one of his fighters too.

Anyway he's forced to send me, he has no choice, everyone's in danger. He needs us all, he can't save anyone, not me or the other young kids (because everyone's young), and not even Mira. Mira's his girlfriend, his good and beautiful companion. They've been in love since before the war, done everything and been through everything together, lived, demonstrated, campaigned, trained, traveled, resisted, stirred up revolt, wept, celebrated. They've always fought, fought, fought with no hope of victory, but without despair. She believes in it too, she smiles too. She's lovely, Mira, with her almond eyes, always cheerful, full of energy. She sweeps through the ghetto streets like a tornado, her boots striking the ground with a purposeful stride. She's small, almost frail, in her too-big sheepskin coat, but her talk is full of passion, her laugh full of life, and she's full of love for him and he loves her too.

So do I . . .

8

"Jews, the Occupier Is Preparing"

Jews, the occupier is preparing
the second act of your extermination.
Don't go passively to death.
Defend yourselves!
Take an ax, a piece of iron, a knife.
Barricade yourselves.
By fighting you have a chance of salvation.
Fight!

They're coming back!

On January 18, 1943, the Germans launched another Aktion. Once again, arrested Jews are lined up and taken to the Umschlagplatz. But this time, they're not alone. Ten fighters, including Mordechai Anielewicz, are mixed in

41

with one of the groups that march heads down, terrified and helpless, to a horrible and inevitable death . . . when suddenly Mordechai gives the signal, a grenade is thrown at a guard, Molotov cocktails explode, shots are fired, and Nazis fall. The Jews escape in all directions, while the Germans and resistance fighters kill each other. Unfortunately, nine of the latter group die, but they die in battle, they die standing. Only one escapes. Mordechai!

You can't kill him . . .

There are other attacks, other deaths, other escapes. Enough so that after four days, the Germans stop the raid and leave again.

So can we? Make them retreat? Defeat them, scare them? Even win? It's good to have a little hope again, to be allowed to dream a little. That the war will end, that they'll never come back, that we'll live a long time . . . To dream that we'll live!

Mordechai is happy. When he talks with people in the ghetto streets, he senses they have changed: their eyes are bright, more full of life, and he's proud. Now everyone believes not in victory but in having a choice. All are determined to fight for their lives, or for their dignity— they're one and the same. Of course, most cannot fight and besides, there are so few weapons . . . But at least Mordechai knows that at the critical moment, the entire ghetto, for sure, will be able to resist by fighting or hiding.

In the following weeks, preparations intensify. The largest possible number of fighters must be armed and taught to shoot. Strongpoints must be set up in cellars and attics. Communication routes must be created throughout the ghetto, underground passages through cellars and sewers, walls knocked down between attics for movement between adjoining buildings. Quick, quick, we have to be ready . . .

Ready for the evening of April 18, 1943, ready for Mordechai's last speech, ready for his words of bravery, his declaration of war. He says the time for revolt is finally here and tomorrow the end will begin. Our goal is not to win but to fight to the death, a chosen death, not one that is forced upon us. He says, and it makes us cry, "I don't know if we'll see each other again, but at least we'll die having done everything we could."

His voice is calm and strong, the look in his eyes gentle, determined, and his pale, slender hand strokes his revolver. He's our angel, our avenging angel, a general and a dreamer who is leading us into an impossible war. The war of several hundred children armed with pistols against thousands of helmeted, booted, armored soldiers.

Us alone against the German army. We're doomed, but not despairing.

We're going to win this losing battle.

We're ready.

9

"We Succeeded"

*We succeeded beyond our
wildest dreams!*

And it's the morning of April 19, 1943.

The sky is blue, the air smells fresh, it's spring-time in the ghetto.

During the night, while Nazi soldiers surrounded the wall, Mordechai Anielewicz went from apartment to apartment, check-ing that everyone was at their stations. He was calm as ever, giving us courage, incentive, confi-dence. Nobody slept—too much excitement and exhilaration, too much eagerness to fight. The instructions are simple: shoot and then die, kill as many Nazis as you can before being killed. But that doesn't scare us, it doesn't make us sad.

There is so much life in us, so much joy and pride, it's like happiness, like hope!

And now we're waiting for the Germans. When will they come, when will our end begin, our end in a blaze of glory? Suddenly we hear rumbling, pounding, a roar: they're here, they're coming in, a real army, a disciplined horde, two thousand men of war, an entire battalion with uniforms and polished boots, equipped with machine guns, submachine guns, tanks, handguns, and planes, led by General Stroop, the SS commander sent to crush us. They advance through the streets of the ghetto, crying out their songs of blood, as if proud of a conquest, sure of our defeat.

And opposite them is us, the ghetto army, an army of children, an army of orphans; seven hundred boys and girls between thirteen and twenty-four years of age, ragged, starving, and barely trained, led by a frail student; armed with three hundred and fifty revolvers, ten rifles, ninety grenades, a few hundred Molotov cocktails, explosives, and two mines.

And that's all.
But we shall overcome!

What is Mordechai thinking, just before launching his beautiful losing battle? Is he thinking of his parents, who won't see him in his moment of glory? Is he thinking of revenge, does he feel hatred for those he will kill, who've killed so many of us, the ones who are advancing now to finish us off? Is he thinking of the future he will not see? Of our lives that have barely begun and too soon will end? We are with him, around, in front of and behind him, confident and determined. Surely he feels proud because we're so young and we're going to fight. Surely he's sad because we're so young and we're going to die. Mordechai, Mordechai, are you happy, is it wonderful to be here, is it amazing to be you at this poignant instant before you set off the Warsaw ghetto uprising?

Now!

He raises his hand, ignites the fire, hurls thunderbolts, avenges hate, washes away sorrow, touches the sky, changes history, saves the world!

At his signal, a fighter stationed near a window throws the first grenade into a column of Germans passing in the street. It explodes—oh, sweet sound!—and that is the magic moment of our resistance! Our shots ring out from all sides, our grenades explode, and under our gunfire Nazis fall to the ground, injured, calling for help; panic-stricken, they yell, back away, and beat a retreat.

We hear them shout in amazement: *"Juden haben waffen,"* "The Jews have weapons," it's like a song, a poem, an ode celebrating our revolution, our resurrection. It's the first time they've seen Jews armed, and the first time we've seen Germans fall. So they can bleed, cry, and beg too? So we can injure, kill, and crush them too? What a joy it is to fight on our feet in broad daylight, to defend ourselves as Jews, finally strike back! We are no longer hunted animals, we've become human beings again, we're fighters, and they're the ones who are afraid and flee, dying.

All day we throw and we shoot, and they shout and they flee. We lure, we chase, we trap, and we kill. "We have to kill as many as possible," says Mordechai with his kind voice, to catch up a little with the thousands and millions of ours they have killed, tip the scales of death, so desperately unbalanced.

And in the evening they run away! The Germans are fleeing us! They leave the ghetto, knowing they've lost, they leave defeated.

And we're alive!

10

"We'll Exhaust the Enemy"

We'll exhaust the enemy by
attacking nonstop, day and night, from behind doors,
windows, and ruins. Our plan is to take
advantage of the ghetto labyrinth.

Mordechai Anielewicz is happy. Everything went well, he had everything perfectly organized. The Germans suffered heavy losses and withdrew— it's more than he dared hope for! During the fighting, no house was taken and the fighters, despite their tender age, showed themselves to be valiant and brave. Everyone's happy that it's begun, and everyone's cheerful despite the bloodshed. And though I didn't kill because I'm not armed, I still feel wonderful for having been such a help, for having transmitted orders, been the connection, the messenger in a war that we won.

Today.

And tomorrow.

And the day after.

On the first night, some of the kids raised a Jewish flag on the roof of a building. Look, look! A star fluttering over the ghetto! Not the star of shame that tarnishes our sleeves, not the star of hatred they engraved on our foreheads. This star is proud, it's beautiful, it's our lucky star. It repairs our wounded hearts, soothes our humiliated souls. This flag means we have a country, the country of our pride; it means we're a living people worthy of respect. That's what we have won. So we won.

It's good to wake up on the morning of April 20 and still be alive. We didn't think there would be a tomorrow! Mordechai smiles, he says he didn't expect to see this morning, see that sun and that flag, he didn't think he'd still be here!

But he's alive, we're all alive, more than ever, if not for long, and proud to continue, to fight till the end.

During these three days of fierce combat, we are the strongest, we whom they called subhuman against those who believed they were superhuman. We have the advantage and we hold on to it, we control the fighting. It is we who decide when, where, how, what, and who, again and again, ever stronger! Mordechai directs operations, giving orders and answering questions from the fighters who flock around him. His technique is simple, it's the one he applied in the streets of his childhood and adolescence when he fought against the young anti-Semitic Poles. Lure the enemy into an ambush, drive them into a corner, the back of a courtyard, attack by surprise and give them a pounding. Like street kids—but that's what we are, living and dying on the street!—we stay on the move, mobile, unpredictable, and launch surprise attacks left and right, catching them unawares and making them panic. When he was little, did Mordechai know he was already preparing for this struggle, learning to fight this battle, that he had already started this revolt?

The Nazis are scared, they hide, they hug the walls. The arrogant masters of the cruel world don't dare show their faces or enter the buildings where we hide. They shout at us to come out, but we don't. They tell us to give ourselves up, but we don't. "Never," says Mordechai. They don't understand where we got all these weapons from, all the rifles that are firing at them. But we have only one that we pass from house to house so they'll believe we're heavily armed . . . They're shocked to see that there are even women, with beautiful glowing faces, who shoot with both hands and hide grenades in their underwear!

And in the evening they withdraw, they retreat, they leave again, and we stay, and we win. It's hard to believe but so good to see the all-powerful Nazi army fleeing from a handful of little Jews!

April 19, 20, 21, three beautiful days of pure

joy and jubilation, of not believing it's true: their defeat, our strength, the miracle occurring, the children's victory over the German ogre.

11

"In the Name of the Millions"

*In the name of the millions of
Jews who have already been murdered,
on behalf of the ones who are fighting so
heroically, and on behalf of all who are
condemned to die, we call out
to the whole world.*

And then they start the fire.

By the twenty-second, despite our determination, we are beginning to suffer from the imbalance of forces and resources. There are so many of them, with so much reinforcement, so many heavy and light weapons, in the sky and on the ground. And our numbers are dwindling and we can hope for nothing, no, there won't be anyone coming to help us. We are running out of weapons and grenades, and our little fighters are dying one by one. Yet even now, we are making the Germans leave.

On April 23, Mordechai Anielewicz and his staff move into a large bunker at 18 Mila Street, one of six hundred underground shelters, well camouflaged and well equipped. From now on, orders to different combat groups will come from here; it's here that decisions will be made about when, where, and how an action must be carried out. It's also here that liaison officers like me are sent, bringing messages, instructions, and news. The bunker is full of activity, people going in and out; it's the hub of the action, the heart of the ghetto, beating hard.

But also on the twenty-third, the Germans change tactics. On that day and every day thereafter, they stay outside the gates of the ghetto. From outside, well protected from our paltry weapons, they attack us with shells and flamethrowers, and the ghetto goes up in flames. The fire gains ground daily, spreading from one neighborhood to the next.

The fire wins.

For how can we fight? What good are weapons when there are no more enemies? What good is courage in the middle of a fire? Mordechai is surprised, caught off guard. He didn't expect the Germans to choose fire instead of bullets, refuse confrontation, and liquidate us without our being able to retaliate. He feels cheated, frustrated: where is his beautiful battle of man against beast, with the Germans in the role of the beast? How can anyone stand tall and proud in this raging fire that burns our eyes, ignites our clothes, slowly suffocates us? Faced with fire, he is—we are—powerless.

And we're trapped. When the walls collapse on people, when there are no more staircases and the windows explode, we'll have to get out, but where can we flee to? Some jump out the windows clutching small children, their little treasures. But they get shot; from the other side of the wall the Germans are practicing their shooting, hunting the flying Jew, and the bodies are already shattered by the time they hit the ground. Other people cling to the balconies and scale the walls like small animals, trying to get up to the attics. There are those who flee into the streets; on melting sidewalks, among corpses, they run screaming through hell.

Meanwhile on the other side of the wall, it looks as if a party's going on, it's paradise!

Through collapsed sections of wall, on the Polish side, through black clouds of smoke you can see a sparkling merry-go-round, girls in bright skirts, whirling children living their radiant children's lives. Through our death cries and cannon fire, the barrel organ can be heard singing its song of life, the one we used to sing too, and there is the sound of laughter. Where they live, children are laughing.

Only a few yards separate us, and yet they are

light-years, fire-years away. The wall between us divides the world in two. Our world is black and white and theirs is in color, where they live it's spring and where we live is hell. We are dying so close to them, yet they look as if they don't even see or hear us. As if for them we don't count, we don't exist. Only the black butterflies of our lives on fire drift across and land on the flowered dresses.

They're right next door! And they're letting us burn! They don't come help us, it doesn't make them cry. They shed no tears and don't take up arms.

And the merry-go-round turns and the ghetto burns . . .

12

"Our End Is Near"

Our end is near.
But as long as we have weapons,
we'll continue to resist.

May 1 arrives . . .

All the survivors have been hiding for over a week now, trapped in overheated bunkers. They can't fight anymore, the only alternative is to die in the flames or fall into the hands of the Germans. And Mordechai Anielewicz blames himself for not foreseeing this possibility, for not planning an escape. His goal wasn't to survive but simply to stay alive long enough to kill as many Nazis as possible. But since we can't fight anymore, he regrets not digging tunnels or exploring the sewers so we could escape and try to join the Polish partisans in the forest.

I sometimes see him standing off to one side, tired and even discouraged. What is going through his mind as he stands there alone? Regrets, desires, a mad longing to live? Sorrow, too many tears, the desire to end it? Hatred and blood, the urge to destroy everything? Is he sad because he's going to die? Because we're all going to die? Does he ask himself what it's all worth, does he want to stop? Does he regret pulling us into it? Does he think that because of him . . . does he think he should have . . . that if not, maybe . . . that alas, it's all over?

Does he remember the summer camp in the Carpathian Mountains in the summer of 1939? Mira and all his friends were there. They laughed and joked around so much, the counselors criticized them for being irresponsible and undisciplined. In the intense heat of the bunker, does he dream of the mountain, the cool early mornings and the fragrance of the evening? Does he remember how he ran in the forest and held his beautiful companion, and that he was free and believed in his freedom? Does he regret the future he thought he'd have, all the things he'd do, the happiness that awaited him? Does he mourn the children he'll never have?

Mordechai, do you remember the world before the end of the world?

I saw him last night alone in a corner, his eyes were closed, I think he was crying. Does an angel cry? Does he lose his wings?

But even in tears, Mordechai doesn't despair; even without wings he can still fly. He turns his despair into strength, into courage, into goodness. Regardless of his doubts, he knows how to get us involved, and encourage us even when he's discouraged. He's the perfect leader, not only because of what he is, but also for what he's made of us. We shared everything with him, struggle, fear, joy, hunger, dreams, fire, and soon death. But we don't regret anything: it was worth it, worth the pain.

So much pain . . .

He's a respected leader, everyone obeys and trusts him. Despite the danger, the chaos, and the end that is drawing near, he keeps us disciplined and united, bound by feelings of fellowship, friendship, love. Nobody has any family left, we are each other's family, each of us watches over the other, and Mordechai watches over all.

He's a friendly leader, caring and gentle. He gives orders kindly, distributes tasks fairly. He never stops, but remains calm and serene. I love to see him talking crouched down among his commanders, going from group to group and joking to boost the morale of those who are worried, smiling a sad but genuine smile. Tonight, as he does every night, he shakes hands with each fighter who's leaving on a mission, he makes a joke and says goodbye, and everyone's afraid it means goodbye forever. When they get back in the early morning he gives them a warm hug and listens as they excitedly tell him about how they escaped danger. He tends to the injured, and like all the rest of us mourns the dead.

For despite the spreading fire and our dwindling munitions, operations continue. When evening falls, the patrols go out among the smoking ruins to look for food and bring back reports on what is happening. They visit other groups, transmit orders, report positions, greet friends, look for the missing, do the body count. It's dangerous. Walls crumble, floors cave in, flames consume, smoke asphyxiates, mines explode. And the Germans are never far, lurking, watching, shooting. *They* have weapons, food, and all the time in the world. But night scares them and there aren't so many of them in the ghetto then, so we only go out after dark.

Except on May 1.

The beautiful blue morning of May 1.

The day before, Mordechai recalled his long years as a militant and told me about them with nostalgia. Though for months he's been fighting for an honorable death, he hasn't forgotten that before, he was fighting for a just life. Helping others to live as human beings and helping them die are part of the same struggle against those who deny human dignity.

Yes, we're prisoners, we're doomed. But he insists that for one last time we celebrate May 1, the day that honors freedom and hope for the future. No parades, no music, no red flags, but the way we did before: all together, fists raised with brio.

Then comes morning and it's time for the attack in broad daylight, as in the first glorious days. Scattered among the ruins, we raise our weapons and jubilantly fire our last bullets, standing proud and happy because in spite of everything, it's beautiful to die under the blue sky, killing Germans, on the first of May.

The last May fades away . . .

13

"Soon, Very Soon"

Soon, very soon, I'm going to a place
where nobody wants to go, and from which
no traveler ever returns.

And then it ends.

All over the ghetto in flames, the ghetto in ruins, methodically, day after day and one by one, the Germans locate the bunkers. With weapons or gas, they force people out to kill them or arrest and deport them. One by one until ours, at 18 Mila Street, the heart of the revolt, Mordechai's refuge with one hundred and twenty fighters. On May 7, it finally happens; the Nazis find us, surround us, and block all exits.

We're trapped.

We can't leave, can't breathe, and the heat is

unbearable. Outside the Germans wait, inside we suffocate. Crushed together, sweating and gasping, we wait for death, which will come tomorrow for sure, in the morning. The last night is long, the last night is sad, because it's the last. We always knew it would end, that we'd have to die. But it's sad for life to end when it's only just begun; it's terrible to die when you're not even twenty. We haven't lived our lives! Everyone is silent, wracked by sorrow.

Mordechai is silent too. He's solemn, of course, but at the same time so proud. Twenty days, it lasted twenty days! He would never have dared hope that we'd hold out so long! Twenty days of life gained, of honor regained. We have nothing to be ashamed of. He feels sad, of course, but not hopeless. Breaking the heavy silence, he says to a girl: "Sing us something. Our lives must end with a song." She begins to sing a song from the time before, and the sweet words bring us a little comfort, the beautiful notes are a lullaby for the last night, whispering goodbye.

But on the morning of May 8, all our music stops, replaced by the sounds of Nazi drills above our heads. They bore little holes and send down their suffocating gas to poison us. And soon the air in the bunker is no longer air at all.

This time, it's over, there's no more hope. It's impossible to escape, and surrendering is out of the question. Mordechai announces that it's time to die. But we won't let them take our lives: we'll do it ourselves because our lives belong to us, and because they're sacred. We will give ourselves death by our own hands. With dignity.

So Mordecai and all his companions raise their weapons and turn them on themselves. They shoot their youth, put an end to their lives, kill themselves slowly, and one by one they die.

To see them fall breaks my heart.

Suddenly, just as the Germans are about to enter the bunker, a voice cries, "Over here! A way out!" Just before I flee, I turn and see Mordechai lying on the ground with Mira, his body abandoned, face hidden. I call out, weeping, but he doesn't answer, and he doesn't move, and he doesn't get up.

He will never live again.

We've lost our angel, our soul, our great and beautiful commander! But he won his war.

He died with honor, he died in battle. He died a man with dignity, a free man, a hero.

He died a human being.

He died.

Mordechai!

14

"My Life's Dream Has Come True"

My life's dream has come true.
I'm happy to have been among
the fighters of the ghetto.

With a few fighters, we were able to escape through stinking sewers, crawling for hours on end without knowing where we were going. We finally emerged and fled, drunk with freedom and grief, to join the Polish partisans in the forest. For a few more days, isolated shots rang out from the heaps of ruins in the ghetto, fired by the last survivors.

On May 16, General Stroop announced: "The former Jewish quarter of Warsaw is no longer in existence."

Of the seven hundred JCO fighters, none went voluntarily. Only a dozen survived.

Our revolt lasted twenty-eight days. Up against the powerful German army, we held out longer than either the French or Polish army.

And yet, we were just a troop of children, innocent, heroic, who went to war against Germany to save our souls, led by a young man, pure of heart, heartbreakingly gentle, incredibly brave.

He was a good man, a decent man, a *mensch*.* He was able to rise up, full of light in the middle of darkness, and in terrible times he led a desperate struggle without despair.

His name was Mordechai Anielewicz.

He was an angel . . .

---

* In Yiddish, a "decent man."

Afterword: They Too Said No

Despair is an inherent part of the human condition. All beings, all groups, all peoples and eras have faced it at one time or another in their history. This can be individual despair caused by bereavement, loneliness, poverty, separation, illness, failure, or depression. It can also be collective despair that affects a community, a social group, or a country or people suffering from injustice, persecution, exploitation, famine, war, or extermination.

We can sink into this despair. But we can also say no, refuse to give in to it, and fight to stay on our feet, to live or die with dignity. People engage in this fight in many circumstances, extreme and tragic, or far more modest and benign. It takes a variety of forms, ranging from armed struggle to humor, from solidarity to poetry, scientific research to rebellion.

The revolt of the Warsaw ghetto is the ultimate expression of saying no to despair. Mordechai Anielewicz and his companions knew they had no chance of winning. Starting in 1939, Hitler and the Nazis invaded Europe and carried out a reign of hatred and violence. They considered Jews subhuman and wanted to "rid" the world of them. Everywhere Jews were subjected to countless restrictions and humiliations, one of which was wearing the six-pointed star. They were grouped together and isolated in closed areas called ghettos, where a great many died of starvation and disease. The largest of these was the Warsaw ghetto, where nearly four hundred and fifty thousand Jews were crowded into less than two square miles, trying to survive in appalling conditions of hygiene and malnutrition. In January 1942, at the Wannsee Conference, the Nazis decided to implement the "Final Solution," that is, the extermination of all the Jews in Europe. They deported them to concentration camps, gassed them in gas chambers, and burned them in crematoria. The largest of the extermination camps was Auschwitz-Birkenau in Poland. It was at the Treblinka camp that the Jews of the Warsaw ghetto were murdered after they were arrested during the great Aktion of summer 1942. In all, nearly six million Jews and two hundred and twenty thousand Romani, along with countless Slavic and German Communists, anarchists, the disabled, gay people, and others from groups considered "unfit," perished in what have been called the death camps.

It was in this context of absolute horror that Mordechai Anielewicz and his comrades conducted their hopeless revolt. They knew they could not force the Germans to stop the extermination of the Jews. They knew that no one would come to their rescue, neither the Poles nor the

Allied forces, and that not one of them, or very few, would manage to survive. Yet they decided to resist for the sole purpose of resisting, and fought their battle for life to the death.

In the wake of the Warsaw ghetto uprising, other armed revolts broke out. There were insurrections in many Polish ghettos, in Vilna, Krakow, Bialystok, and also in Lithuania, Belarus, and Ukraine. Uprisings also occurred in concentration and extermination camps, though these were ruled by terror and a total lack of freedom. In August 1943 at Treblinka, in October 1943 at Sobibor, in October 1944 at Auschwitz-Birkenau, emaciated prisoners rebelled and attacked Nazis with makeshift weapons.

Almost all were killed.

Throughout the war, there were many other isolated acts of resistance. A scattering of admirable, courageous individuals rose up against their tormentors, cursed at them, spat in their faces, leapt upon and attacked them with their bare hands.

The Warsaw ghetto uprising echoes another heroic struggle, that of the Masada. In the year 73 CE, after years of struggle against the Romans who occupied their country, the Israelites had taken refuge in Masada, their last stronghold on the cliffs above the Judaean Desert. After several months of siege, knowing the end was near, their commander, Eleazar ben Ya'ir, gathered his soldiers and exhorted them to commit suicide rather than fall alive into the custody of their enemies. And so nine hundred and sixty perished by their own hands, having set fire to all their possessions except food to show that they hadn't been defeated by famine due to the siege but that they'd chosen death rather than slavery, preserving their ultimate freedom and depriving the Romans of the pleasure of victory. When the Romans entered the fortress, they met only silence.

Throughout the history of humanity, we find examples of people who have stood up to a far more powerful enemy and refused to give in to despair. Between 1915 and 1918, up to two million Armenians were exterminated by the Turks. Missak Manouchian was only eight years old when he saw his father leave at the head of a group of Armenians to fight the Turks in a losing battle and be killed on the hills above Adiyaman. Was it the beautiful memory of his father that prompted Missak, who'd become a poet and was living in France, to join the resistance in 1942 with the FTP-MOI*? What hope did they have, all these resistance fighters in the shadows who initiated actions against the occupier, starting in 1940? Isolated, working underground, could they have believed they would defeat the German army, which had crushed all other armies? But they did not hesitate, and their acts of bravery played a part in the final Allied victory against the Nazis. A victory that Manouchian did not

---

* Francs-tireurs et partisans—main-d'œuvre immigrée (Partisan irregulars of the MOI—Immigrant Workforce Movement) Branch of the Communist Resistance (1940–1945), primarily made up of foreigners

witness because he was shot at Mont-Valérien in February 1944, along with his Affiche Rouge comrades. But true to his father's example, he died resisting.

So did the 147 Communards, lined up in front of the Federates Wall and shot on May 28, 1871, after attempting to establish the Paris Commune in a popular uprising against the government of Versailles. The insurgents wanted Paris to be governed by the people and aspired to establish a number of social reforms. The Commune lasted two months and ended in bloodshed.

In Tiananmen Square in Beijing, in June 1989, blood was also shed: that of Chinese students who were peacefully demonstrating for democracy and died crushed by government army tanks. They also remained standing until the end, proud and true to their ideals.

In America, the history of the enslavement of Africans and African-Americans and genocide towards indigenous peoples is a history of unending oppression and ongoing resistance, including the oppressive Jim Crow laws and transformative Civil Rights Movement in the 20th century, and the Black Lives Matter movement in 2020.

Over the centuries, many men and women have rebelled against miserable and oppressive conditions, demanding greater social justice and dreaming of a free and egalitarian society. They campaigned, demonstrated, fought, sometimes at the cost of their lives, to try to change a world that seemed unchangeable and all-powerful. Of course, this fight for a better world is not finished and remains very much a part of our lives today.

Any act of resistance is a no to despair. To say no to despair is to refuse the unacceptable, rebel against the inevitable, challenge the insurmountable, fight the invincible.

It is to believe in life despite all opposition.

Rescuers who tirelessly search for survivors in rubble after an earthquake, doctors who try to pull the wounded and ill out of the jaws of death, volunteers who help to rebuild a country in ruins are also part of this struggle against despair.

This fight is not only collective. It is also personal, everyday, intimate. Everyone fights in their own way, when they must, as they are able, acting, giving, and defending themselves, campaigning, creating.

In the late nineteenth century, Helen Keller, a young American woman, deaf, non-verbal, and blind, seemed doomed to living cut off from the world but engaged in a struggle to learn to read, write, and speak. Those who don't become resigned when confronting a disability also demonstrate a refusal to give in to despair.

Humor is an effective weapon against despair, as is art in all its forms. In the concentration camps, some prisoners recited poems to one another so as not to lose their humanity. But even in less extreme conditions, music, litera-ture, or painting help people continue moving forward when the future seems blocked, help them to smile in the midst of distress, when all hope seems lost.

In the Bob Dylan song entitled "Let Me Die in My Footsteps," the following lines capture something of the spirit of Anielewicz and his fellow resistance fighters:

"I will not carry myself down to die,

When I go to my grave, my head will be high."

To say no to despair is doing what you have to do in any circumstance: stand tall and be a good person, a decent person. A human being, quite simply. That is what Mordechai Anielewicz was. Long after his death, he continues to live on in the streets of Warsaw, in these words that I write, in your heartfelt memories.

Chronology

1919: Mordechai Anielewicz is born in Wyszkow, Poland, to a poor Jewish family.

1930s: He joins the ranks of Hashomer Hatzair, a socialist Zionist youth movement.

September 1, 1939: The troops of Nazi Germany invade Poland, signaling the start of World War II.

1940: Mordechai Anielewicz organizes resistance groups among Jewish youth in occupied Poland.

November 15, 1940: The Warsaw ghetto is sealed off.

January 20, 1942: The Wannsee Conference takes place, where Nazi leaders decide to implement the "Final Solution to the Jewish Question," i.e., the extermination of the Jewish people.

Summer 1942: Three hundred thousand Jews are deported from the Warsaw ghetto, most of them to Treblinka extermination camp.

November 1942: Mordechai Anielewicz becomes commander of the Jewish Combat Organization.

April 19, 1943: The Warsaw ghetto uprising starts.

May 8, 1943: Mordechai Anielewicz commits suicide.

May 16, 1943: The Warsaw ghetto uprising ends.

May 8, 1945: Germany surrenders, marking the end of World War II in Europe. Between 1939 and 1945, six million Jews have been assassinated.

For More Information

FILMS:
The Time of the Ghetto, Frédéric Rossif, 1961
The Island on Bird Street, Søren Kragh-Jacobsen, 1997
Uprising, Jon Avnet, 2001
The Pianist, Roman Polanski, 2002
Seven Minutes in the Warsaw Ghetto, Johan Oettinger,
    2012

BOOKS:
The Little Boy Star: An Allegory of the Holocaust, by
    Rachel Hausfater and Olivier Latyk, Milk & Cookies
    Press
The Island on Bird Street, by Uri Orlev, HMH Books for
    Young Readers
28 Days: A Novel of Resistance in the Warsaw Ghetto, by
    David Safier, Feiwel & Friends
The Complete Maus: A Survivor's Tale, by Art Spiegel-
    man, Pantheon Graphic Library

LINKS:

www.yadvashem.org
  Yad Vashem: The World Holocaust
  Remembrance Center

www.gfh.org.il/eng
  Ghetto Fighters' House Museum

encyclopedia.ushmm.org/content/en/article/the-
    warsaw-ghetto-uprising
  Article on the Warsaw Ghetto Uprising

www.ushmm.org
  United States Holocaust Memorial Museum
  Washington, DC

www.mjhnyc.org
  Museum of Jewish Heritage
  New York, New York

www.museumoftolerance.com
  Museum of Tolerance
  Los Angeles, California

Kibbutz Yad Mordechai in Israel is named in memory
  of Mordechai Anielewicz.

Discussion Questions

"The opposite of despair is not hope. It's struggle." Do you agree?

Mordechai Anielewicz said: "Rebel against reality!" What did he mean?

Do you think fighting is, in certain circumstances, the only solution?

Although the insurrection was defeated, the ghetto fighters won their battle for human dignity. Is human dignity important? Why?

The Warsaw ghetto uprising is a symbol of heroism. Why is it exemplary?

Feigele participates in the insurrection, although she is only fourteen. What do you think of child "soldiers"?

While the ghetto was burning, Polish people went on with their lives on the other side of the wall. Do you think they should have tried to help? To what extent are witnesses responsible?

Mordechai Anielewicz "led a desperate struggle without despair." In what ways did you see him drive away despair?

Have you ever said no to despair? In which circumstances?

Saying no to despair "takes a variety of forms, ranging from armed struggle to humor, from solidarity to poetry, scientific research to rebellion." Give examples that you have witnessed or heard about.

"I will not carry myself down to die,
When I go to my grave, my head will be high."
Discuss these words from Bob Dylan.

About the Author and Translator

Inquisitive and often on the road, RACHEL HAUSFATER has lived in Germany, the United States, and Israel plying various trades. Today, in addition to writing, Rachel Hausfater is an English teacher at a school in Bobigny, France. A translator and author for Thierry Magnier publishing, she wrote a novel in 2009, *Un soir j'ai divorcé de mes parents* (*The Night I Divorced My Parents*).

ALISON L. STRAYER's translation of Annie Ernaux's *The Years* won her, in tandem with the author, both the Warwick Prize for Women in Translation and the French-American Translation Prize and was shortlisted for the International Man Booker Prize. Strayer's translation of *Infidels* by Abdellah Taïa was longlisted for the Albertine Prize, and her co-translation of *Rencontres fortuites* by Mavis Gallant was shortlisted for the Governor General's Award for Translation. Strayer's novel, *Jardin et prairie*, was shortlisted for Canada's Governor General's Award for Literature and the Grand Prix du livre de Montreal. She lives in Paris.